Eugenie Fernandes  Henry Fernandes

ORDINARY AMOS AND THE AMAZING FISH

Scholastic Canada Ltd.

For this book, Eugenie did the layouts and the rough drawings. Henry did the finished drawings and painted them with acrylics and coloured pencils on Strathmore paper.

This book was designed in QuarkXPress, with type set in 20 point Comic Sans.

Scholastic Canada Ltd.
175 Hillmount Road, Markham, Ontario L6C 1Z7, Canada

Scholastic Inc.
555 Broadway, New York, NY 10012, USA

Scholastic Australia Pty Limited
PO Box 579, Gosford, NSW 2250, Australia

Scholastic New Zealand Limited
Private Bag 94407, Greenmount, Auckland, New Zealand

Scholastic Ltd.
Villiers House, Clarendon Avenue, Leamington Spa,
Warwickshire CV32 5PR, UK

Canadian Cataloguing in Publication Data

Fernandes, Eugenie, 1943-
Ordinary Amos and the amazing fish

ISBN 0-590-51737-6

I. Fernandes, Henry. II. Title.

PS8561. E7596O72 2000   jC813'.54   C99-932291-5
PZ7. F47Or 2000

5 4 3 2 1   Printed and bound in Canada   0 1 2 3 4 /0

For each other.

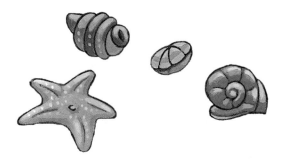

Amos was an ordinary man.
He lived in an ordinary house
by an ordinary pond.
He had an ordinary chair, an ordinary cat,
and an ordinary fireplace to keep him warm.

Amos lived an ordinary life.

Every day was the same.

He got up.

He went fishing.

He came home.

He went to bed.

And that is how it was.

One day, as Amos was fishing in his ordinary boat, something extraordinary happened.

Amos felt a strong pull on his fishing line.

He held on tight.

"Holy smoke!" he cried.

"What an amazing fish I am catching!"

The fish pulled Amos this way and that,
all over the pond.

"I'll fry it in butter with salt and pepper,"
shouted Amos.

The fish pulled harder and harder.

"No," cried Amos. "This one's a trophy!
I'll take it home and hang it on the wall."

But that is not what happened.

Amos did not catch the fish.

The fish caught Amos.

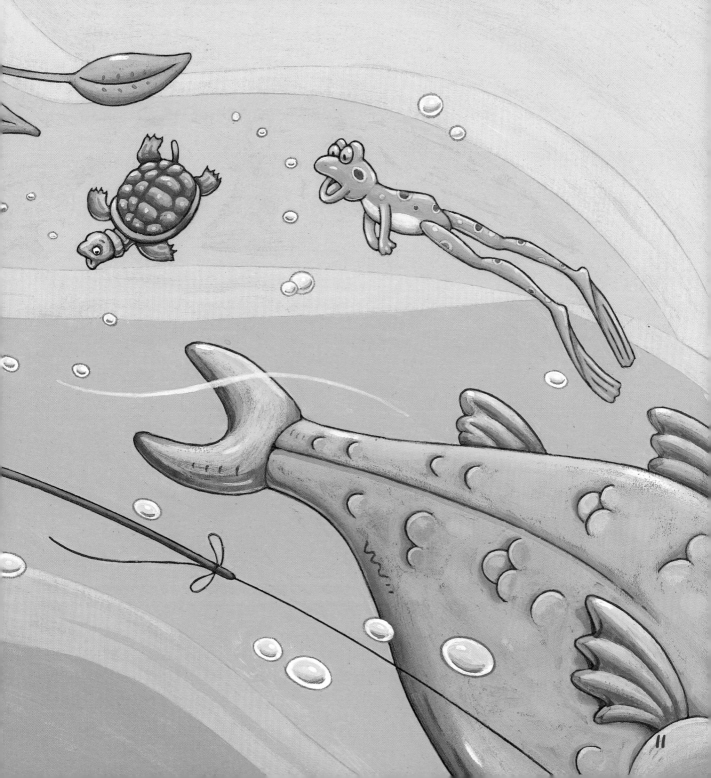

The fish took Amos home
and showed him to his wife.
"I'll fry it in butter with salt and pepper,"
she said.
"No," said Father Fish. "This one's a trophy.
I'm going to hang it on the wall."
"Oh, no," cried Little Fish. "I want him for a pet."

"What about the last person you had for a pet?"
said Father Fish. "You didn't take care of it,
and you know what happened."
"I know," said Little Fish. "But this time I'll take
good care of the person. Please may I keep him?"

Father Fish looked at Mother Fish.

"Well . . . all right," she said.

"But I'm warning you, Little Fish.

If you don't take care of this person,

I'm going to throw him back."

Little Fish was happy.

He got a person bowl and filled it with air.

Then he put Amos inside.

After several days,
Mother Fish said to Little Fish,
"The person looks tired.
Why don't you give him a chair?"
So Little Fish gave Amos a chair.
It was much more comfortable than
the chair that Amos had at home.
Amos sat down and fell asleep.

When Amos woke up,
he heard voices
outside his person bowl.
"May I hold him?"
asked Cousin Fish.
"Better not," said Little Fish.
"He might bite you."
"He looks hungry,"
said Grandmother Fish.
She gave Amos some food.
It was much tastier than
the food that Amos had
at home.
Amos ate it all up.

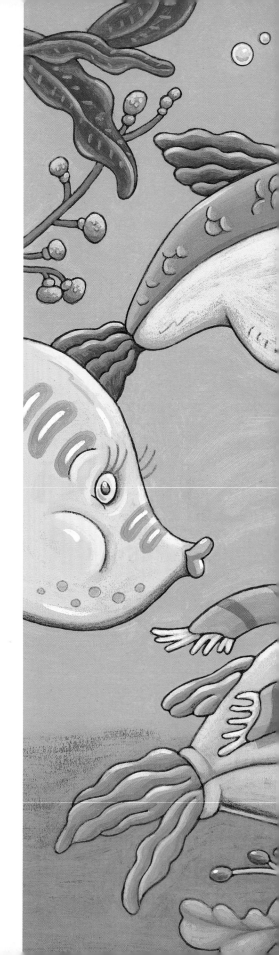

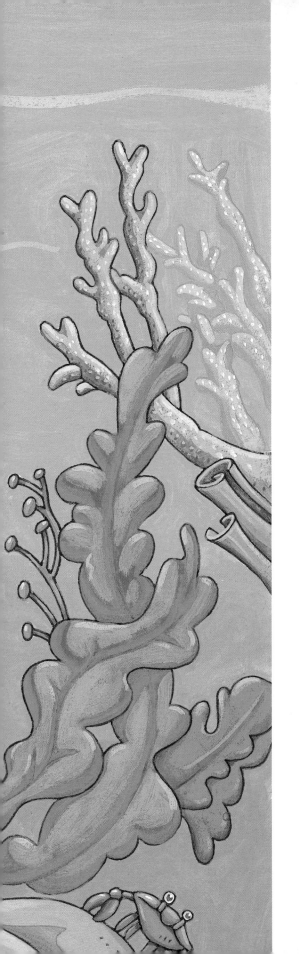

"He looks chilly,"
said Grandfather Fish.
So he built a fireplace for Amos.
It was much fancier than the
fireplace that Amos had at home.
Amos sat by the fireplace
to get warm.
"Now he has a perfect home,"
said Little Fish.
But Amos was not happy.
"I don't belong here," he said.
"I wish I were back in my
very own, ordinary home."

Uncle Fish looked at Amos and said,
"I had a person once, but he got old and he died."
When Amos heard this, he began shouting
and leaping around his person bowl.
"He needs to calm down," said Little Fish.
"Maybe we should leave him alone for a while."
And so they did.

Days passed, and the fish forgot all about Amos.
Even Little Fish forgot about him.

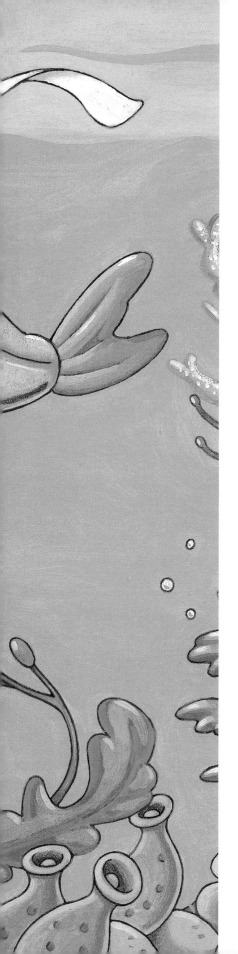

Amos grew weak and tired and bored.
His beard grew down to his ankles.
His clothes became tattered.
Garbage piled up around his chair.
His fire went out.

One day, Mother Fish found
Amos looking sad and limp.
"I knew this would happen," she cried.
"That Little Fish has done it again.
He's just too little to care for a pet."

With that, Mother Fish took Amos
out of the person bowl and threw him back.
Amos went flying up out of the water
and into the bright sunlight.
He flew over the treetops
till he landed with a plop
at his very own front door.

Amos jumped up and hugged the house.

He hugged the flowers. He hugged the trees.

He ran inside and hugged the chair.

He lit the fire and kissed the cat.

The cat was happy. Amos was happy.

"Look at this chair. Look at this cat.

Look at this fireplace," cried Amos.

"This isn't ordinary. This is wonderful!"

And that is how it was.